# The Little Slipper Man

A story by
Manfred Kyber
with pictures by
Monika Laimgruber

Hamish Hamilton

Once there was a little man. He was very small, and he was also invisible, so that no-one could see quite how small he was. It was not worth seeing him anyway, because there was really nothing special about him. He just walked around by himself, and that was all there was to him.

The grass witch, who had magical powers, had seen the little man, because she could cast spells and see all invisible things. "It is not really worth seeing him," said the grass witch. "He is quite small. He has a little head as round as a potato, and thin stalky legs like a grasshopper. He just walks about by himself all the time, and that is all there is to him. There is nothing more to be said."

©1971 Artemis Verlag. English translation ©1972
Hamish Hamilton Children's Books Ltd. First published
1971 by Artemis Verlag, Zürich. First published in
Great Britain 1972 by Hamish Hamilton Children's Books
Ltd. 90 Great Russell Street, London WC1B 3PT All
rights reserved. SBN 241 02129 4 Printed in Switzerland
Reprinted 1974

The little man was furious. He wanted to be seen, and he wanted people to talk about him. He ran to the market, where a fat woman sat beneath an umbrella and traded in shoes and slippers. The little man put on a pair of enormous slippers, into which his stalky, grasshopper-legs quite disappeared, and he walked off.

The market woman did not notice anything until she heard a shuffling noise, such as mice make. She looked up, and saw two of her biggest and most beautiful slippers walking off down the street by themselves. The market woman cried out in amazement, and had to drink three pewter mugs of hot coffee before she recovered her wits.

"Look at those walking slippers!" all the people shouted, and they stopped to stare as the slippers went by. What was the world coming to! To see such huge and beautiful slippers, the best the market woman had, walking off by themselves with quick and busy steps, was astonishing indeed. No-one could believe their eyes.

Muffie Snufflebeard, the wise tomcat, was sunning himself on the window sill. "Slippers that walk by themselves!" he said. "There must be some small creature inside them and if I could only see him I would eat him. It shouldn't be allowed." Muffie Snufflebeard, the wise tomcat, sniffed suspiciously and licked his own honest paw as he watched the slippers go by.

The little man was pleased by all the commotion he was causing. "Now at last I am somebody and everyone can see me," he said, and he swelled with pride, turning his round potato head this way and that.

But nobody could see the little man at all, only the slippers, even though the little man ran faster and faster and the slippers flip-flopped on his stalky grasshopper-legs.

He ran with ease in the wide street, which was just right for slippers and shoes, but when he came to the meadow where flowers bloomed and the street ended, it seemed to him that the going was not so easy. He wanted to be seen and admired in the meadow, too, but it is one thing to run down the wide street in flip-flopping slippers, and quite another to trudge through the bumpy meadow. The slippers were only comfortable in the streets of the town, and not in the meadow where magic begins, and everything is quiet, and even Muffie Snufflebeard goes about on silent paws.

Poor little slipper man! He took a huge leap into the sweet-smelling grass, his slippers flew off, and he landed head first in a mole hole.

The grass witch and her cousin the meadow frog pulled the little man out of the hole. And it was just as well that they did, for the mole would surely have had something to say about it. Even someone who is invisible can be a nuisance if he is stuck in your front door.

The little man wandered off into the green grass, and no-one ever saw him again. There was really nothing special about him. He just walked about by himself, and that was all there was to him.

The slippers were found by an owl, who took them to his home in a hollow tree at the edge of the forest. The owl put the slippers side by side, and there they stayed as the finest and most comfortable beds Mr. and Mrs. Owl had ever had. By the light of his lantern eyes Mr. Owl read his newspaper, curled up cosily in his slipper bed. He never again suffered from rheumatism in the claw, for the slipper kept out the cold.

The toad, who lived at the foot of the tree, just nodded her head. "I knew all along it would end like this," she said. "After all, our meadow is full of magic. It isn't just an ordinary street, for anyone who wants to slip-slop about in slippers." And she went on knitting herself a cardigan of moss.

Toads always seem to know about everything before it happens, but they don't always tell until afterwards. And anyone can do that.